CLAUDE

on Holiday

ALEX T. SMITH

HODDER

At 112 Waggy Avenue, behind
a tall front door with a big
brass knocker, lives Claude.

4

'The author is a comparative newcomer to children's books; on this evidence, he should go far.'
The Independent on Sunday

'A handsome creation.'
The Children's Bookseller

'Perfect for newly developing readers and great to share.'
Primary Times

'Watch out for this new kid on the children's books block, you will be won over!'
Librarymice.com

'I loved everything about this book.'
Bookbag

For my Dad,
Master of the Terrible Joke

HODDER CHILDREN'S BOOKS

First published in Great Britain in 2011 by Hodder Children's Books
This edition published in 2017 by Hodder and Stoughton

16

Text and illustrations copyright © Alex T. Smith, 2011

The moral rights of the author and illustrator have been asserted.

A CIP catalogue record for this book is available from the British Library.

ISBN 978 0 340 99901 1

Design by Alison Still

Printed in China

The paper and board used in this book are from
well-managed forests and other responsible sources.

MIX
Paper from
responsible sources
FSC® C104740

Hodder Children's Books
An imprint of
Hachette Children's Group
Part of Hodder and Stoughton
Carmelite House
50 Victoria Embankment
London EC4Y 0DZ

An Hachette UK Company
www.hachette.co.uk

www.hachettechildrens.co.uk

And here he is now.

Claude is a dog.
Claude is a small dog.
Claude is a small,
plump dog.

Claude is a small,
plump dog who
wears a beret and
a lovely red jumper.

Claude lives in his house with two
people who are too tall to fit on this
page. They are called Mr and Mrs
Shinyshoes, and they both have
very shiny shoes and neat ankles.

6

Every morning, while Claude is
tucked up in his bed, Mr and Mrs
Shinyshoes whizz around the house,
getting ready to go to work.

Sometimes Claude watches them
with his beady eyes and sometimes
he just pretends to be asleep.

Then at half past eight on
the dot, Mr and Mrs
Shinyshoes put on their
coats. 'Be a good boy, Claude,'
they say. 'We'll see you later!'
And off they pop to work.

Once the front door has closed behind them, Claude leaps out of bed. He puts his beret on his head and fishes his best friend, Sir Bobblysock, out from under the blankets. It is time for an adventure!

Sir Bobblysock

Where will Claude and
Sir Bobblysock go today?

11

One morning Claude had
a brilliant idea.
'I think I will go on holiday!'
he said.

Sir Bobblysock decided he
would come too, as he had
been very busy lately and felt
like a rest.

Claude had never been on holiday before, so he didn't know quite what he was meant to do. He thought it would be a good idea to take all sorts of interesting things with him, just in case they came in useful.

So he pulled out a suitcase from under his bed and started to pack.

He put in some underpants and a tambourine. He added some suncream and some squirty cream in a can. He popped in a lampshade, some sticky tape and a selection of slightly squished sandwiches.

15

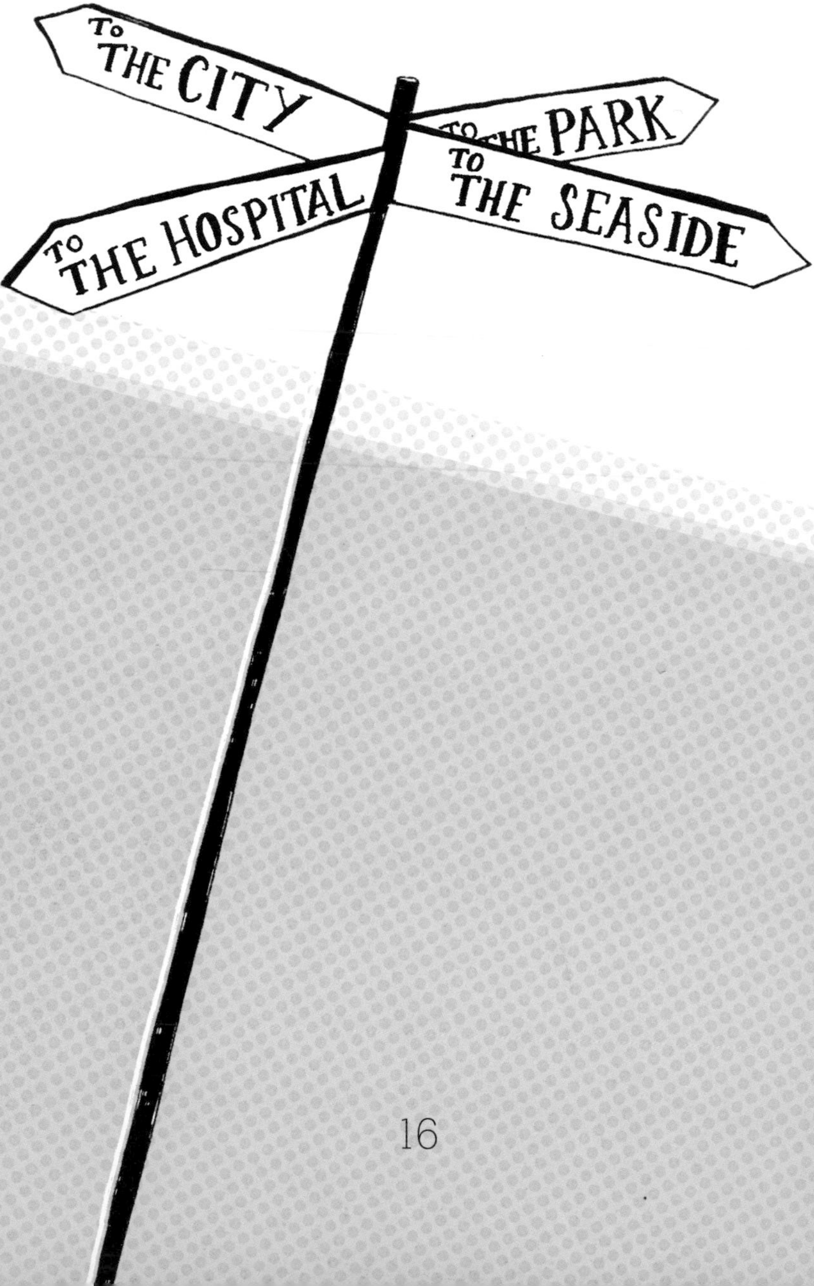

TO THE CITY

TO THE PARK

TO THE SEASIDE

TO THE HOSPITAL

Then Claude clicked his suitcase
closed and set off for the seaside,
with Sir Bobblysock hopping
along behind him.

It was very busy at the seaside.
There were people sunbathing
or sitting in deckchairs, and
children shouting and playing all
over the place. Everyone seemed
to be in their underwear!

Sir Bobblysock settled
down on his towel, popped
on his sunglasses and
immediately fell asleep.

Claude thought he had better try
to fit in, too. He opened up his
suitcase, took out the pair of
underpants he'd packed and
pulled them on.

Unfortunately, the underpants
belonged to Mr Shinyshoes,
so they were much too big
for Claude!

He stood scratching his head
for a moment, wondering how
to keep them up, before he
remembered he'd packed some
sticky tape...

22

Ah, that was better.

It was a lovely sunny day. Claude fancied getting a tan, but he knew that the hot sun could burn him if he wasn't careful. And although he liked the colour pink, he would clash dreadfully with the wallpaper back at home if he got burnt.

Along the beach he saw a man
squirting cream all over himself.
Claude thought he would copy
him. He got out his suncream and
his squirty cream and set to work.

25

Firstly, he covered himself in suncream, from the tip of his nose to the toes of his sensible shoes. He rubbed it in very carefully. Then he gave the can of squirty cream a quick shake. He squeezed out a big frothy dollop of cream on top of his beret.

Now Claude was ready
to start having fun.

But before he could enjoy strutting
up and down the beach in his new
swimming trunks, he heard a shout
from somewhere out at sea.

28

Claude spun around and
squinted towards the direction
of the noise. He gasped!

A man was splashing wildly about
in the water – and just behind him
was an enormous shark!

Claude looked about to see where the lifeguard was. He and Sir Bobblysock had seen programmes on television about emergencies like this. He knew a lifeguard should be diving into the water to help.

But the lifeguard wasn't. He was helping somebody with her beach balls.

Claude tutted and rolled his eyes. Calmly, he reached under his bcret, found his armbands and popped them on. Then he dashed towards thc sea and jumped into the waves.

Claude had won awards for his doggy-paddle, so it didn't take him long to get to the scene of the emergency.

Claude tapped
the enormous shark
on the fin and cleared his
throat. 'It is not very nice to
eat people,' he said. 'A juicy bone
baguette is much more delicious.'

And he took his emergency
bone baguette from
under his beret.

The shark looked very surprised.
Then the shark looked very pleased
indeed. He took the juicy bone
baguette gently in his gigantic teeth
 and swam off, as happy as anything.

'Hold on to my tail please,'
Claude said to the
splashing man, and
together they doggy-
paddled back to shore.

39

Everyone on the beach had been watching very closely, and they were all amazed by Claude's bravery. When Claude splashed back on to the shore with the rescued man, they cheered.

'HOORAY!' they cried.

Everyone except Sir Bobblysock,
because he was still fast asleep
on his towel.

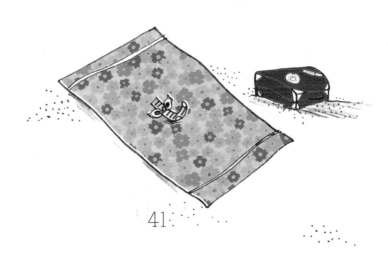

After all that excitement Claude
was beginning to feel a bit peckish
himself. It was nearly eleven
o'clock, after all.

Usually he and Sir Bobblysock
had a nice cup of tea and a jam
tart for their elevenses. But as
he was on holiday today, Claude
fancied something more exotic –
like an ice cream, perhaps.

He woke up Sir Bobblysock
with a prod and together
they strolled to the shop.

The shop was full of French
people, who had come to the
seaside for their holiday.

They were all speaking French.

Oh! Un petit chien!
*Oh! A little dog!

44

45

'Of course!' thought Claude. 'On holiday, you have to speak another language.'

So Claude decided to copy them. He pulled out his phrase book from under his beret and asked for two ice creams in what he hoped was French.

The shopkeeper didn't seem to understand, so Claude tried again – more loudly this time.

Excusez-moi, 'ave you une glace à flavour of juicy bone?

*Claude hoped this meant 'Excuse me, do you have any juicy bone flavour ice cream?'

The man behind the counter was utterly perplexed and decided to just give Claude three enormous ice creams, a rubber ring and a large flag all for free!

Claude and Sir Bobblysock left the shop slurping their ice creams, feeling very pleased with themselves.

49

After they had finished their mid morning treats, Claude wondered what else they could do on the beach. He looked about and saw some children making sandcastles.

It looked rather fun so he decided to make his own. Sir Bobblysock joined in too.

After about an hour, Claude had finished his sandcastle. He was very pleased with it.

He looked over at Sir Bobblysock's effort...

'Some people are dreadful show-offs,' thought Claude sniffily.

Then he noticed someone with a
clipboard looking carefully at all
the sandcastles. She stared at Sir
Bobblysock's for a long time.

It turned out they had accidentally entered a sandcastle competition, without even knowing it – and Sir Bobblysock won first prize! It was a pair of snazzy flip-flops! Claude put them under his beret for safety.

55

Claude and Sir Bobblysock were resting on their towel when they saw some interesting-looking people, stumping along the sand towards them.

'Arrrrrrrrrrrrr!' cried their leader, licking a lolly. 'We be lookings to look for some treasure, so we be!' And he flapped a treasure map at Claude. 'Will you help us, matey?! I be Porthole Pete, I be, and this be my crew, Slopbucket Stu and Deadeye Denise.'

57

Sir Bobblysock, who knew about these things, thought that they might be pirates.

But Claude thought looking
for treasure sounded fun, so he
nodded politely, packed up his
suitcase and followed
Porthole Pete to
the seashore.

A piratey-looking ship, The Damp Dog, was bobbing about happily in the waves.

Sir Bobblysock was very doubtful about the whole idea. In the past, he had suffered badly from sea-sickness – but he tutted and followed Claude anyway.

The treasure map showed
there was an enormous
chest full of goodies
hidden nearby on
Skull Island.

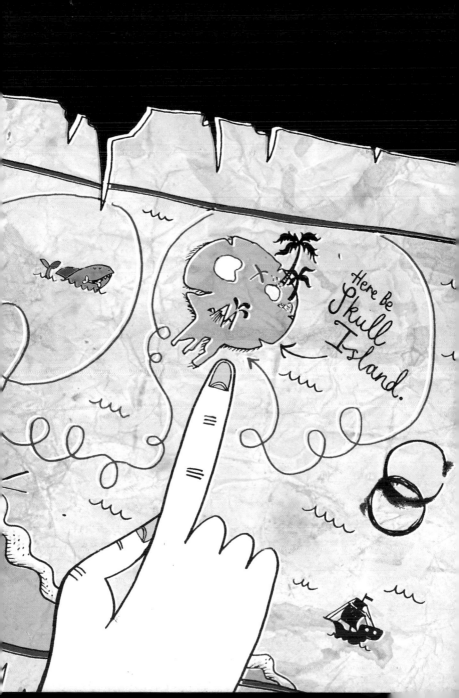

Claude and the pirates splashed along at a terrific pace. Sir Bobblysock found the sea rather unsettling. He spent most of the time lying down in a cabin with cucumber slices over his eyes.

After a few minutes, they
arrived at the island and began
looking for the treasure.

Claude, Sir Bobblysock and
the pirates looked:

under rocks,

around palm trees,

and down holes,
but the treasure was
nowhere to be seen.

67

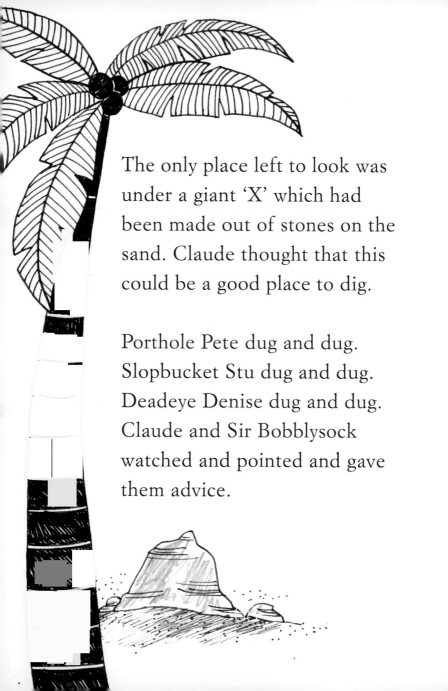

The only place left to look was under a giant 'X' which had been made out of stones on the sand. Claude thought that this could be a good place to dig.

Porthole Pete dug and dug. Slopbucket Stu dug and dug. Deadeye Denise dug and dug. Claude and Sir Bobblysock watched and pointed and gave them advice.

Before long there was a
deafening CLANG! which gave
Sir Bobblysock a headache and
made Claude's ears wobble.

Claude and Sir Bobblysock
looked into the deep, dark hole
that had been dug...

'HOORAY!' they cried.

They had found the treasure!

Quickly, they pulled the chest
out of the sand and started
scampering back to their ship
with it. But they hadn't got very
far before they heard a cry!

'Oh no!' shouted Porthole Pete. ''Tis Naughty Nora, the fearsome naughty pirate, and all her naughty crew! Run!'

So Claude, Sir Bobblysock and the crew of The Damp Dog started to run, but...

UH-OH! Claude tripped.

76

They were surrounded.

Claude started to feel a bit sweaty under his collar. Sir Bobblysock could feel his heart beating in his ears.

Naughty Nora strutted up to Claude's suitcase and had a good snoop inside.

78

She looked at the lampshade,
she looked at the tambourine,
she looked at the squirty cream.

'Hmm...' she said.

'Captain?' said one of the
naughty pirates. 'Don't we need
a new lampshade for our ship,
cos you wore our last one as a
hat and then we lost it?'

Naughty Nora nodded slowly.

'And we could do with a new tambourine,' said another naughty shipmate, 'cos you used our last one as a tray for afternoon tea and then we lost it.'

Naughty Nora nodded again.

'And we could do with some more squirty cream,' said the first naughty shipmate, 'cos you took the last lot on a picnic and then – '

'Yes, all right!' snapped Naughty Nora.

The other pirates watched silently as Naughty Nora stood frowning, looking from the treasure chest to the suitcase and back again. She sniffed one of the slightly squished sandwiches.

'We will swap you our treasure chest for your suitcase full of interesting and useful things!' she said.
'Deal?' And she held out a hand for Claude to shake.

Claude looked at Porthole
Pete and Porthole Pete
looked at Claude.
Then Claude
nodded politely
to Naughty Nora
and shook
her hand.

Before the Naughty pirates could change their minds, Slopbucket Stu had flung the treasure chest on top of his head, and the crew of The Damp Dog skedaddled back to their ship.

'Hooray for Claude!' shouted the pirates. 'Hip, hip hooray!'

Claude looked at his feet and went a bit red. Sir Bobblysock made a low bow.

''Ere, matey!' cried Porthole Pete, as he opened the chest and plunged his hands into all the gold.
'Why don't you and Sir Bobblysock come and join us full time 'ere on The Damp Dog? You be makin' great treasure hunters, so you be!'

But Claude was feeling
tired – going on holiday was
more exciting than he had
ever imagined. So he and Sir
Bobblysock said their goodbyes
and made their way home with a
beret FULL of treasure.

That night, when Mr and Mrs
Shinyshoes came home from work,
there was sand all over the place.
Mrs Shinyshoes was sure she could
smell a whiff of seaweed.

'Where on earth has all
of this treasure come from?' asked
Mr Shinyshoes, biting one of the
gold coins to see if it was real.

'I don't know,' said Mrs Shinyshoes.
'And I'm not even going to ask why
there's a pair of your underpants here,
covered in sand!'

Claude and Sir Bobblysock
pretended to be asleep. It
would be their little secret.

Interesting and Useful **French Words**.
These words might help you next
time you go to the seaside:

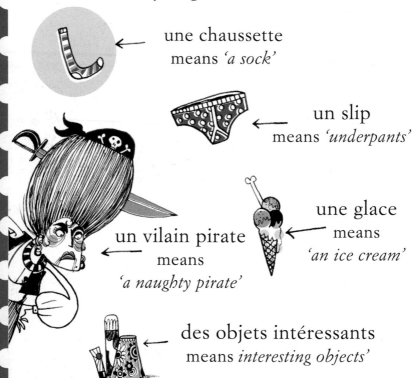

une chaussette
means *'a sock'*

un slip
means *'underpants'*

une glace
means
'an ice cream'

un vilain pirate
means
'a naughty pirate'

des objets intéressants
means *interesting objects'*

And remember to keep you eyes out for
Claude and Sir Bobblysock. You never
know where they might pop up next!